# The Seekers

A Dark Story of the North

by
Brendan Myers

NORTHWEST
PASSAGE
Books

The Seekers

ISBN (Print edition): 978-0-9920059-8-6


Published by
Northwest Passage Books
Gatineau, Quebec, Canada

For all enquiries, please visit the author's web site:
BrendanMyers.net

## ~ **Acknowledgements** ~

In April and May of 2014, the Fellwater series of novels was the subject of a successful fundraising campaign on Kickstarter.com, a popular internet-based crowd-funding platform. More than five thousand dollars was raised from 144 supporters to pay for professional editors and designers.

I wish to thank all of my project backers for their generosity and support, not only with their money, but also with their time promoting the project. In particular, I wish to thank these outstanding benefactors and world-builders, each of whom donated $100 or more to the project: Carole Martin, Ben Rossi, David LeBer, Gary Gibson, Laurent Castellucci, David LeClerc, and Ezekiel Zong-Han Azib.

The Seekers

When the truck ran out of road, the driver shut off the engine and closed his eyes, and remembered what silence sounded like.

Ibrahim Nefzawi wrapped his numb fingers in his armpits and bowed his head. Ghazwan nudged him, to make sure he didn't fall asleep.

Ibrahim sighed, and tried to be cheerful.

"Well, it's time for us all to do the bravest thing we have ever done in our lives," he said.

"What's that?" said Fred.

"Step out of the truck."

Ibrahim was rewarded with sardonic laughter. He and his two brothers had been driving together since the early morning, in the cramped cabin with their bulging packs of winter gear. It was not a comfortable journey. Their shoulders were pressed into the sharper parts of backpacks and snowshoes. The heater broke shortly after they began driving, so they had bundled into their coats and huddled under blankets. Hands were frantically rubbed together. Hot coffee was taken at every opportunity. Jokes in bad taste were told to pass the time. So when the wheels of their truck spun uselessly against a bank of hardened snow, they were glad of it, but they were also trading one kind of hardship for another.

"You couldn't give us two more minutes," said Fred. "It's winter out there."

Ghazwan elbowed him roughly and said, "We've been sitting in this little metal box for the better part of two whole days. I want to go for a walk."

"So do I," said Ibrahim. "We might have two days of walking still ahead of us. So let's not put it off any longer. I'm opening my door in five seconds. Everybody ready?"

The brothers nodded; Fred unhappily.

Ibrahim counted to five, and opened the door.

Winter instantly invaded the truck and robbed them of what little warmth they had hoarded there. The brothers howled and cursed for the loss of it. They quickly fell out of the truck, and happily waved their arms, and jumped up and down, and threw snowballs at each other and kicked the snowbanks, glad to be free. Then they wrapped themselves in their blankets again.

"So." said Ghazwan, "Two days of walking?"

"Maybe more," Ibrahim replied, as he surveyed the snow that covered their path.

"Why couldn't we have waited until the summer, to come up here and look for the old man?" Fred complained.

"Because we need him *now*," Ibrahim answered. "He's the oldest of all the Secret People in Canada. Maybe the oldest in the world. Miranda says we need his help."

"You should have told me before we left that he was hiding *this far* north," Fred muttered, as he untied some of the bags from the back of the truck.

"Would you have come if I told you?"

"Hell, no."

"That's why I didn't tell you."

Fred glared at his brother, muttered something, and then continued unpacking the truck.

Ghazwan was standing on top of the cab, surveying the surroundings with binoculars. "Snow, in every direction, out there," he reported. "Trees covered in snow, and rocks covered in snow, and ice covered in snow, and snow covered in snow! If I didn't know better, I'd say the snow goes on forever, and we are standing on the edge of the world."

"Maybe we are," chuckled Ibrahim.

"I'm not even seeing any trails. No skidoo tracks. No animal tracks. It's like we are the first living things to set foot here."

"I bet we'll be the last," muttered Fred.

As Ibrahim unloaded a sled from the truck, he said, "Let's camp here for the night, and get walking in the morning."

\*     \*     \*

The biggest pack they unloaded from their truck held their tent. Ibrahim smiled as he opened it and tossed its contents on to a patch of snow that he had swept and flattened. The little bundle of wooden poles and canvas sheets rolled into the centre of the clearing, under its own power. Then it unfolded itself and spread out. The ropes scuttled about the sheets and threaded themselves into rings on the edges. The poles unfolded and lengthened themselves, and hooked themselves on the ropes, forming a ring. Then the ring raised itself up, and the ropes pulled the canvas sheets in place. Not a moment later, a large and comfortable Mongolian yurt had fully erected itself, and the front flap opened to invite the brothers inside.

"God, but that was hard work," Ibrahim laughed.

The brothers buried the tent walls up to its roof in snow, for insulation and for protection from the wind. When they were finished, Ibrahim took out a long wooden pole from the back of the truck, attached a blue and white flag to it, and raised it beside the tent. His brothers chuckled to see it, although Fred also shook his head.

"What did you bring that for?" he asked Ibrahim.

"Because, I respect what it stands for. The blue for the sea, and the white for the desert, for the great empire that our ancestors once ruled in West Africa. The swords, because they were warrior kings, proud and strong. And the moon above the swords, for the Ummah; because of our submission to peace. It seems good to me that anyone we pass on our expedition should see that we stand for such things."

"We're not going to meet anyone out here," Ghazwan predicted.

"Even so," Ibrahim added with a grin, "with this flag planted here, we can pretend that this tent of ours is part of our old madrasa, and we are not so far from home."

Fred only rolled his eyes, but said nothing. Ghazwan stifled his laughter.

The brothers climbed into their new home away from home, buttoned the front flap closed, draped a blanket in front of it, rolled out a few small carpets on the floor, and set up a small kerosine camping stove in the centre. When they finished their work, they saw that it was good. They huddled in a circle around the stove, with blankets over their shoulders. They warmed some beans and a pot of soup on its flame, and ate quietly.

"I met him, once, you know," said Ibrahim. "The Old Man, that is. Before he went missing."

"Is that why Miranda sent you to find him?" asked Ghazwan.

"Probably," Ibrahim guessed. "Maybe she thought he would remember me."

"What was he like?"

"He was – it's hard to say, it was so long ago – he was cheerful, he was generous. Quick to laugh, and his laughter was loud. But he was also sad, and quiet sometimes. He could recite the Arabian Nights, word for word, from memory. And all of the Rubayat of Omar Khayyam. In the original Farsi! When he walked into a room, it was like the sun and moon came with him. He loved us all so much. But he would leave a gathering early, sometimes without saying goodbye. Sometimes he wouldn't leave his house for ten straight days. He loved his life, he loved this world, but he loved his loneliness, too."

Then Ibrahim stared at the ceiling of the tent, remembering.

Fred prodded him and said, "So the man loved us, but he ran away. All the way up here. Sounds like a man who really wants to be left alone."

"We need him. We need his knowledge. A man who has reached his great age has learned a thing or two about life. I respect that. And so should you, Fred."

"I'm not impressed," Fred drawled. "Seriously. Why are we here? Is there a war coming? What's the point?"

"Exactly," said Ibrahim.

"What do you mean, 'exactly'?" Fred countered.

"Think about those questions you just asked. They're not only about our search for the old man. They're also about your life, and mine, and the life of everyone around you. What if there was someone in the world who discovered the final answers to all the biggest questions? The man we've come north to find might be that man. He's been living on a hilltop, hundreds of miles away from everywhere, doing nothing but talk to the earth and the sky, for fifty years! A man who could do that must surely be a great man."

"Or a great idiot," snickered Fred.

"I want to meet him. I want to learn from him," Ibrahim finished, and his gaze wandered off to the distance.

Fred put his soup bowl down and said, "There's another story about why he left us. It says he was a self-absorbed know-it-all, and he left because no one would worship him."

Ibrahim raised an eyebrow at Fred. "That's the first time I've ever heard anyone speak of him like that," he said.

"I met him too. Just once, but it was enough. He asked me why our mother named you Ibrahim, after the prophet, and why you're called Ghazwan, the conquering hero, and why I'm just Fred. Of all the stupid names a man of our great house could bear!"

"He never judged or dismissed people like that. He was a great man."

"I'm sure he was a man, but I doubt that he was great."

"That's enough arguing, you two," Ghazwan said. "Don't let the cold and these cramped quarters get on your nerves."

Fred and Ibrahim sat back in their seats, like boxers sent to their corners.

"Why did you agree to come on this expedition to find him?" asked Ibrahim.

Fred shrugged his shoulders. I didn't know we'd have to come so far north. Now, I'm going outside to piss."

Ibrahim and Ghazwan quickly threw their blankets over their heads to protect themselves from the blast of cold that invaded their tent, as Fred threw back the flap and stepped outside.

"What's his problem?" Ibrahim asked Ghazwan.

"Cabin fever, probably," Ghazwan sighed. "Want some more beans? Farting in your sleeping bag will help keep you warm."

Ibrahim waved Ghazwan's beans away with a smile.

"I never met the old man, myself," Ghazwan related, as he spooned some more beans into his bowl. "But I've met a few others who have. And they say, that in the last few months before he went up north, he was losing his mind. Talking to shadows. Eating stones and grass. Forgetting his own name. One day he went down to a lake to have a bath. But he was gone so long that his friends went to look for him. When they found him, he was in some kind of shock. He couldn't speak. Something had frightened him so badly, his hair had turned all white. The very next day he got on his horse and came up here. For a long time after, if you said someone was going up north, it meant that he was going insane."

"So if you think the old man is mad, why did you agree to come find him?" Ibrahim asked.

"Because you're my brother, and you asked me for my help."

Ibrahim smiled, and put his hands on his brother's shoulders, and they touched their foreheads together.

*   *   *

After their meal, they piled their blankets and pillows on their sleds, up off the floor, lest the frozen earth suck away their body heat in the night. Fred and Ghazwan found sleep easily, but Ibrahim struggled. In his mind, he he could still hear the noise of the engine from the day's road trip. And Fred was snoring. In the morning, Ibrahim was the first to get up. He bundled into his coat and leggings and boots, took the flashlight, and went outside.

The winter greeted him with an achingly cold breeze, which seared his face and froze his breath on his beard. It also gave him a perfectly quiet dawn, and a sky blue-black in the West and cyan in the East, with a glaze from a low moon, and a landscape of smooth and clean blue-white snow, and everything tinkling with the last of the morning stars. Except for the occasional crack of some ice and a shifting of some snowbank somewhere, all was quiet, hushed, and pensive. The few small bare trees, little more than standing twigs, marked the snowfield like jagged black headstones over the graves of foolish men who thought they could conquer this land by force. Yet, as little trees, frozen still, but still alive, they testified to the perseverance and the will of earthy life, which comes to a hard land, tests its footing cautiously, and finds a way.

Much as he found the sight inspiring, soon Ibrahim also found it cold. So he decided that lying awake in his bed and listening to Fred's snoring was preferable to freezing to death. Halfway back to his tent, he turned to take in one last picture of the land, to hold in his memory. Then he followed his footsteps back to his camp.

Ghazwan and Fred were awake and waiting for him there.

"What happened to the truck?" Fred gritted.

Ibrahim looked to the spot where he left it. The only thing that remained was the four tracks in the ground from the four wheels that brought it there. No footprints told of thieves that might have driven it off. Indeed, no tracks told of where it might have driven itself. Ibrahim's eyes bulged in his face.

"Well, that's inconvenient," muttered Ibrahim.

"It can't have disappeared on its own, Ibrahim. So what did you do with it?"

"Me? Nothing! I could accuse the two of you!"

"What? I didn't take it!" Fred snapped defensively.

"Neither did I," added Ghazwan.

Ibrahim looked to Fred and said, "Was it still there when you went out just now?"

"Of course it was!"

"Did you look?"

"Well, no. I had no reason to look."

"Then it might have been gone for hours."

Ghazwan interrupted to say, "It doesn't matter *when* it disappeared. What matters is the fact that it's gone. And so is all the equipment that we hadn't yet unpacked."

The brothers quietly looked at each other as they contemplated what Ghazwan had said.

"Well, it had to be one of the two of you, who made off with it," said Fred, when he could no longer stand the silence. "Look, there's no other footsteps but our own. No footprints coming up the road from someplace else. And I didn't do it. So it had to be one of you."

"Look again, Fred," said Ibrahim, pointing at the tracks. "The only tire tracks in the snow are from when we arrived. There's no tracks from when it drove away." Ibrahim acknowledged the absurdity of the conclusion with a sigh. "I'm only saying, it didn't drive away. It's just – gone."

"It was just an ordinary pickup truck. It wasn't enchanted. It can't just disappear."

"But that's what the evidence is telling us."

Ghazwan and Fred examined the evidence again.

"We can't do anything about it right now. Let's just go back in the tent before we freeze," Ibrahim suggested, and his brothers silently agreed.

They sat in a circle around their camping stove to warm themselves again before getting on with the rest of their day. .

"Nothing we can do about it," said Ibrahim.

"Well I'm going to do something. I'm going to make some coffee," said Fred.

"Why did you go out there?" asked Ghazwan. "It must be minus thirty. You'll freeze your eyeballs open."

"No reason. I just couldn't sleep."

"Did you hear anything? Something that might tell what happened to our truck?"

"I did not."

Fred roughly overturned the sled he had slept on, and howled: "This was such a bad idea, coming all this way. To find what? Some wise guy who will probably shove us off as soon as we find him? This is nonsense. I say we walk south. Let's go home."

"The nearest town to the South is further away than our destination to the North," Ibrahim scolded him. Then he dug a map out of a backpack and laid it out on the floor. "Look. There's Hallowstone Castle, where we started, and there's the road we took that after that. We are right about here, where they close the road for the winter. And here is where we are going. That's where Miranda said we would probably find him. We can hike that in two days. If we went south, we wouldn't even reach the highway in three."

"Well, then, walking there and back, and then walking South again, would make for seven days of walking. How is that better than five?"

Ibrahim and Fred glared at each other, each waiting for the other to capitulate, until Ghazwan broke the stalemate. "We may not have enough food for seven days anyway," he said. "A lot of it was still in the truck."

Fred sat back. Ibrahim closed his eyes.

Ghazwan continued, "I buried two of the coolers in the snow beside the tent. They're probably still there. But they might be all we have."

Fred turned to Ibrahim and said, "I want to say something to you, Ibrahim my brother, because if we die out here, I want to be sure we die with nothing left unsaid between us."

Ibrahim opened his eyes and said, "We're not going to die out here."

"Nonetheless, I have something to say."

"Then say it."

Fred leaned forward and calmly told him, "I hate you."

Ghazwan put down his beans and leaned away from his brothers. His spoon rattled noisily in his empty bowl. The wind outside seemed to slow down, and make the tent uncomfortably quiet.

Ibrahim stifled a small chuckle. "No, you don't," he replied.

"I do," Fred asserted. "I am the eldest. So I should have been made *caliph* when our father died. Instead he passed his turban to you, the youngest. I have known nothing but humiliation ever since."

Ghazwan defended Ibrahim, saying, "Ibrahim didn't choose to be the caliph. Our father chose him."

"Our father chose him because our family joined the Secret People long before both of you were born, but long after me," Fred snapped at him. "That's why you two have hero's names, and I, who was born first, have a name for a fool. And, Ghazwan, I hate you too for the same reason."

Ibrahim response was to clench his fist and grit his teeth, and to say, "You hate me because of my name?"

Fred leaned back again and said, "Because of what your name represents. Because of the life that your name gave to you. That life should have been mine."

Ghazwan decided this was a good moment to say, "It's pointless to argue about who is the caliph. The Guardians took our freehold away from us. Remember? That's why we joined with the Fianna. She is our caliph now."

Fred and Ibrahim remembered.

"Make peace with each other before the cold outside kills us all," Ghazwan told them.

"All right then," said Ibrahim. "Fred, I have something to say to you too."

"Oh really?" Fred grunted. "What do you want off your chest before you die?"

"A promise. That we are *not* going to die," Ibrahim declared. "We may be completely isolated here, with not enough food and no easy way home. But we can still succeed in our mission. And *when* we do, your name will be a hero's name. That is my promise to you."

"I don't believe you!" Fred snapped.

"Be my guest and walk home then!" Ibrahim shouted back, and he pointed to the tent flap.

Fred thought about walking home just to spite his brother. He cast his eyes to the floor, as he thought about what that would really entail.

Ibrahim put his hands gently on Fred's shoulders and said, "We can do this. We can find the old man, and get him back home again. But we have to do it together. If one of us leaves, all three of us will die. But you are my brother, and I want you to live. And I'll tell you another thing. When we find the old man and bring him back home, you will be a hero, and you won't hate me anymore. All will be forgiven, and all will be well."

Fred brushed Ibrahim's hands away. "You're such a cliché, did you know that?" After a breath, he added, "But now that we're short on food we may as well go find the old man anyway. Maybe he has food. And then he can magic us back home, or something."

Ibrahim smiled. "Those aren't a fighter's words, but I'll take them."

Ghazwan was relieved, too. "Miranda gave us a mission. Find the old man. So let's take stock of what we have. Ration our food. And start walking."

As the three brothers organized their gear and cooked their breakfast, Fred asked Ibrahim, "You're not mad that I told you that I hate you?"

Ibrahim smiled, shook his head, and said, "If I stayed angry at you, my own brother, it would be as pointless as staying angry at the whole world."

Fred shook his head, but smiled, and said, "You impossible man!"

\*     \*     \*

The three brothers dressed themselves for a day of walking in the subarctic winter of northern Ontario. Fred and Ghazwan wore toques and hoods; Ibrahim wore a turban embroidered with stars and moons and zodiac signs.

"That turban and parka and sunglasses outfit? Not working for you," Ghazwan said to Ibrahim.

"This land is just a different kind of desert, and just as beautiful to me," Ibrahim replied.

Fred leaned into Ghazwan's ear and said, "He still thinks he's the caliph."

Ibrahim only chuckled, and let the comment pass.

Then the brothers loaded the bags on to their sleds, tied the sleds to their belts with long cables, and tied their snowshoes to their boots, and faced North.

"More than just another desert: this place reminds me of the words of that teacher from House Gautama: 'The truth is a pathless land.' A pathless land. We have left the house of safety, and entered the house of the unknown. In that house, we shall find the truth," Ibrahim whispered.

"Actually," said Ghazwan. "This is Orenda land. They've lived here for centuries. They've put down paths everywhere. But only they know how to see them."

"And I've got a satellite phone and a GPS right here," added Fred.

"Where's your sense of the mythic?" Ibrahim chided them with a grin.

"I left it in the truck," said Fred.

"You left your sense of the mythic in the truck?"

"No, I left my GPS and my phone!" Fred replied, with a worried tremble.

Fred's brothers groaned. Ibrahim gathered his breath and said, "We are three men of House Songhai, the proudest and best warriors among all the Secret People. We can, and we will, complete our mission."

"What, without any clue where we're going? How do we find the old man now?"

"I know how," said Ghazwan. "We look for the signs."

He reached into a pack on his sled, and produced a small handwritten journal, bound in a leather cover, and held closed with a small buckle. "We three are not the first to come up here looking for him," he explained. "About fifty years ago, not long after he disappeared, there was another expedition. And one of the trackers in that expedition wrote this journal. It describes the strange things that they saw in the world around them, as they got closer to the old man's monastery."

"What kind of strange things?" asked Ibrahim.

"Trees in full bloom, in the midst of winter. Great stones and boulders that glowed in the dark. Voices in the air, like old friends from home, begging them to turn back."

Ibrahim asked, "But did they eventually find the old man? What happened to them?"

Ghazwan looked down and admitted, "The journal doesn't say."

"Does it tell us anything useful at all?"

"It says they had an oracle with them, so they would know what signs to look for."

"That's helpful," Fred grumbled. "We don't have an oracle."

"We have this journal," Ibrahim grinned, as he snatched it from Ghazwan. "We can just follow the same signs they followed. And the best sign of all is the fact that this journal made its way back to civilization, and ended up here in our hands. I say that's a sign in itself. It means they didn't die up here. It means they made it back home again! Just like we will!"

"Did they *all* make it back? Or just some of them?" asked Fred.

Ghazwan sighed and admitted again, "It doesn't say."

Fred shook his head, and looked back where the truck had been.

"That doesn't matter," Ibrahim determined. " For we are men of a great and ancient house; men the outsiders once called the djinni-kind; for Allah has awakened our souls. Our ancestors didn't have GPS or sat phones, and they built an empire that covered half of West Africa. We are no less than they were. We can do no less than they did."

"Yes, but they lived in an age of wonders, when the gods still walked the earth," Fred scorned. "They could sense a place of power, hundreds of miles past the horizon. We cannot."

"We don't need to see that far," Ibrahim replied. "All we need to do is follow the story in that journal, and follow the directions in Miranda's map, and take a moment of quiet while we look to the North with second-sight eyes, until one of us sees the path to where the next sign will appear."

Fred said, "So what does that journal say we should look for?"

Ghazwan took back the journal and read for a moment, and said, "The journal says the last sign they saw was a shooting star that flew from the earth to the sky, instead of from sky to earth. So they went looking for the place where it came from. When they got there, they found a summoner, who offered to lead them the rest of the way to the old man's sanctuary."

Ibrahim took a few steps forward, and then stretched his arms and breathed in and out, and looked north. A moment later, he declared that he had found the way, and he started walking.

Fred and Ghazwan looked at each other and shrugged again, and followed him.

"Where did you get that journal?" Fred asked.

"When Ibrahim started talking about this trip," Ghazwan answered, "it was clear that he had a dream, but not a plan. So I called in a few favours."

Fred laughed and said, "You know him well!"

Ghazwan grinned back, and then said, "Better put your sunglasses on, or the snow will blind you."

Fred put his sunglasses on.

*     *     *

The three seekers marched across the white fields, following Ibrahim, who was navigating with nothing but his map and whatever his instincts suggested. He aimed them to the North, or as north as he could figure. Occasionally, he paused to decide which way to go around a grove of short trees or a steep rise in the bedrock. He told his brothers that he knew what he was doing because some routes looked more "right" than others. Sometimes he would ask for quiet from them, so he could feel the destination pulling him closer, and so he would know which way to go. The sun overwhelmed the world with light, and made the snow as brilliant as the sun itself, and cleaned the uncovered trees and stone ledges of any flaws or dissonant marks. All was quiet, and perfect; all that they saw around them belonged where they saw it; and all was appearing to them in peace. Yet they still saw no sign of human life, aside from their own footprints. They still thought themselves traveling a pathless land.

"Jacques Cartier said this was the land God gave to Cain," said Ghazwan.

"Maybe Cain should give it back," Fred snickered.

Ibrahim complained. "Don't spoil a beautiful moment with your sarcasm. If it wasn't so cold, I would think we were seeing the earth as it was the day after it was created. It's perfect. No wonder the Old Man chose to come up here."

"Then let me remind you that whatever stole our truck is still out there," Fred responded.

Ghazwan looked upon the land again with Fred's words in his mind, and the land suddenly appeared ominous and menacing, though nothing about it had changed.

"The old man's monastery is out there too," added Ibrahim. "This is the land where he found the answers everyone is looking for. That makes this land beautiful. That's the correct attitude to bring to a land like this."

Fred only shook his head.

\* \* \*

When twilight arrived, they made their camp in the shelter of a huge glacial erratic rock. They pitched their tent and half-buried its walls in snow as before, and then cooked the last of their breakfast sausages for dinner. For desert, Ghazwan revealed that he had brought the ingredients for mixing vodka martinis.

"You said we were going camping. I thought we could go camping in style," he laughed.

"None for me, thank you," said Ibrahim. "The Book forbids it."

"The Book forbids it? When did you get religion?" said Fred, surprised.

"When I found out that the old man might still be alive," Ibrahim replied, "I thought I should be properly prepared to meet him."

"You don't mind if we-" said Ghazwan, as he mixed the martinis in a thermos. Ibrahim smiled and gestured to show he would not interfere.

Fred said, "There was pork in those sausages, you know."

"No, there wasn't," Ibrahim countered. "I made sure we packed *halal*."

After rummaging around in one of his bags, Ghazwan stood up and said, "Looks like the olives are still in the cooler outside. Probably frozen solid. I'll be back in a moment."

Outside, as Ghazwan searched for his jar of olives, he saw a light, far away, just a hair's width from the horizon. It was lime green, and it flew up into the air, seemingly weakly, and vanished.

"A flare!" he gasped. He darted back into the tent to grab his binoculars. Then he went outside again and frantically strapped on his snowshoes. Then he ran to the highest snowbank nearby and scanned the horizon again. Soon, his confused brothers had joined him.

"What happened, Ghazwan?" asked Fred.

"Did you see a sign?" Ibrahim wondered.

Another flare flew up again, and the sight of it made Ibrahim laugh like an excited small boy. "A shooting star, flying from the earth to the sky! Just like in that journal!"

Fred was skeptical. "It's just a flare."

"Then, it's someone in trouble, and we should go help!" Ibrahim grinned, and he jogged off toward the place where it came from.

The night breeze was stronger when the three brothers were out of sight of their camp. Though running kept them warm, they felt the flash of the icy air on their cheeks and brow and chin. But running in the snow was hard work, even with snowshoes on. First Fred, then Ghazwan, and then Ibrahim got tired, and could not run any longer. Ibrahim leaned on his knees, and caught his breath, and then searched the horizon for another flare. He shouted a few times, but heard no reply. Nor did he hear any echo, or other sign that his voice traveled any further from his throat than the reach of his arm.

A reply appeared in the form of another flare, launched into the sky. The three brothers followed it, and came upon a shallow nook in the earth. A ring of pine trees caught the wind-blown snow and shaped it into a high bank, almost like the walls of a fortress. In the center, sheltered under a rickety lean-to, and bundled in furs and woolen blankets, sat a woman. She lay still, barely awake, but not shivering, as though she had been there for a long time, and was now on the very edge of exhaustion. Long locks of brown hair spilled out from under her hood. In one hand, which might have been turning blue with frostbite, she held a flare gun. When the brothers came close, she trembled, and tried to scuttle deeper into her lean-to, and to load a new flare into her gun. She was weak with cold, and Ibrahim easily and gently disarmed her.

"It's all right, it's all right," he said, in his most reassuring voice. "We saw your flare. We have come to help."

"Not him, not him," the woman whispered, as she pointed at Ghazwan.

Fred and Ibrahim looked at their brother, who held up his hands defensively.

"He won't hurt you," said Ibrahim. "None of us will."

"He is the one the Elder said would come," the woman feared. "The one whose heart is made of ice."

Then she reached for a knife that was hidden in her blankets, and tried to threaten Ghazwan with it, but Ibrahim easily slipped it out of her faltering grasp.

"She must be delirious," Ghazwan imagined. "Look at her. She's hungry, sleep deprived, freezing cold, and who knows how long she's been here all by herself. It must have affected her mind."

The woman shook her head at Ghazwan and said, "No, I know you. I've seen you. I've seen the killing blade in your hand. You are the one he called the Wendigo."

"No, I'm not!" Ghazwan protested.

Ibrahim put his hand on his brother's shoulder. "His name is Ghazwan Nefzawi. He's my brother. This is the first time any of us have come this far North. Whatever it was that happened here, whoever did this to you, it could not have been him."

The woman now changed from panicked to confused. She shook her head. "It's not what he's done. It's what he's going to do. I can see his heart. It's covered in ice."

Fred, who had been standing back and observing, said, "Something else is not right here, guys. Look at what she's wearing."

Ghazwan looked, and said, "A fur parka. Woolen blankets. Oiled leather boots and mittens. Exactly what you need to survive the winter up here. Why does it matter?"

"Now look at what *we* are wearing," said Fred. The brothers looked at their own twenty-first century winter gear, made of synthetic fibers and micro-insulation layers, and realized what Fred was implying.

Ibrahim turned to the woman and said, "My dear child, what's your name?"

The woman hesitated before answering. "Eden Thornhill."

"Eden. I'm Ibrahim Nefzawi. These are my brothers Ghazwan, and Fred, and we are warriors of House Songhai."

"House Songhai?" she said. "But your land is so far away."

Ibrahim smiled, "We are on a mission. Maybe we can help you. Tell me, please, how long have you been stranded here?"

"A few days, not long," she replied.

"And what year is it?"

"What year is it!"

"I know, it's a strange question, but please, what year is it?"

"It's– isn't it 1968?"

The three brothers looked at each other, amazed.

"You say you have been here only a few days?"

Eden nodded.

Fred stepped closer to her and said, "How would you feel if I told you that it's actually 2014?"

Eden shook her head, and then tried to scramble deeper into her lean-to again. "That's not possible, that's not possible!" she repeated.

"Do you know what I think?" said Ibrahim to his brothers. "This woman is a member of that first expedition to find the old man. The one with the scout who wrote the journal."

At the mention of the journal, Eden sat up. "You have Tommy's journal! Then where is he? What happened to him?"

Ibrahim sighed and said, "Nobody knows."

"You killed him and took it!" Eden accused Ghazwan.

"I didn't, I swear!" Ghazwan protested.

"Stay away from me!" Eden shouted.

Ibrahim tried to play peacemaker again. "Relax, Eden, please, relax. Ghazwan could not possibly have killed your friend to get his journal."

"He must have, it's the only way, he must have!" Eden insisted.

"No, he can't have, because the author of that journal disappeared a long time ago."

"That can't be!" Eden insisted. "I saw Tommy here, only this morning. We ran out of food, and he went out with his rifle, to go hunting. It was only this morning!"

Fred tugged on Ghazwan's arm and said, "Is it possible that she's been here all this time, and not noticed the years passing by?"

"I've never heard of such a thing happening before," Ghazwan answered.

"I have," said Ibrahim. "There's a story that the Irish clans tell, about a man named Oisin, who fell in love with a princess of House DeDannan. They went to her freehold, which was on an island in the Atlantic. When he returned, he thought he had been away only three years, but to everyone else, he had been gone for three hundred."

"I know that story," said Fred. "But I don't believe it. There are many places on earth where strange things happen. But *time* is the one universal. None of the gods could change it. Not even the Great Queen."

"There are more things in heaven and earth, Horatio," Ibrahim quoted with a smile.

Ghazwan speculated, "Maybe this girl here has been to a place that makes people forget the passing of time, just like that Irish island."

"Then why didn't she age?" asked Fred.

"Maybe it's also a place that keeps people young. Those Irish islands could do that, too."

"We're not in Ireland. We're in Canada."

"But that doesn't matter," Ibrahim interjected. "Any land anywhere can be enchanted, if only we let the land reveal itself in its own way. Maybe that's why the Old Man came up here!"

"Even if that's true, I don't like it," said Fred. "If this girl here is lost in time, then so are we. And when we get back home, maybe a hundred years will have gone by. Everything will be changed. If that happens, I'm going to blame you, Ibrahim."

Eden interrupted the brothers, though she could do little more than whisper, saying, "Please! I don't know what's happening here. I don't know who you people are or where you came from. But I'm cold, and I'm hungry, and I want to go home. Can you help?"

Eden's plea softened the brothers, and ended their argument.

"I want to go home, too," whispered Fred.

"Well, then," said Ibrahim, "why don't we take you back to our camp? Just as a start, just for tonight. It will be warmer there."

Eden looked at each of the three men in turn, but she looked on Ghazwan with special trepidation.

"I promise you, Ghazwan is not a Wendigo," Ibrahim told her. "We have a little bit of food we can offer you. And we can show you Tommy's journal."

Eden pursed her lips apprehensively. The alternative to accepting Ibrahim's offer was starvation and death in the snow.

"I'm gonna need some help. I don't think I can walk by myself," she said. So Ibrahim lifted her to her feet, and pulled her arm over his shoulder. Ghazwan moved to help, but Eden refused to let him touch her. So Ghazwan motioned for Fred to take his place, which he did, reluctantly.

"I'll do it to help her, and not to help you," he grumbled to Ibrahim.

They hiked back to the tent, with Fred and Ibrahim carrying Eden, and Ghazwan carrying Eden's backpack and blankets.

\*     \*     \*

The four explorers sat in the tent, in a circle around a pot of potato and beef stew that bubbled on their little kerosine camp stove. It was warm enough in the yurt that the three Nefzawi brothers needed only their sweaters, though Ibrahim kept his turban on. Eden wore a flannel nightgown, and hung a blanket over her shoulders. Her hair was stringy and oily from the many days she had spent on her journey, away from home. Bruises and scabs from old cuts and falls dotted her arms and neck and face. Each of the three brothers stole sidelong glances at her when he thought the other two would not notice. In her lap, she held her friend's journal, and as she read it she would sometimes smile or softly laugh, but always with a touch of sadness. More often, she stifled a tear. When she finished reading, she held it to her breast and closed her eyes.

"So, you say it's been almost fifty years," she whispered.

"Do you know how that could have happened?" Ibrahim asked her.

"No," she said. "We were tracking north, looking for the place where the old man said he was going. There were signs in the sky, that he told us we could follow. The kind of signs that used to surround places of power, back in the Mythic Age. There were giants walking in the distance, and white birds that left trails of fire in the air as they flew, and pillars of light reaching up to the stars. There were wonders all around us, and all we had to do was follow them. But it looks like that's all gone now, too."

Eden looked away from the brothers, and rubbed her eyes with her fingers. Ibrahim touched her shoulder, but Eden brushed his hand away. Fred and Ghazwan bent their heads down and ate their stew, and pretended they didn't see that Eden rejected Ibrahim's touch.

Ibrahim tried to say something reassuring. "When we get home, I'm sure everyone will be glad to see you."

"There were twelve of us," Eden related. "Three druids of House Corrigan, who wanted to become the Elder's students. Five scholars of different houses, who had questions they thought the Elder could answer. A scout of the Orenda Nation, so that we wouldn't get lost. A warrior of the Aesir, to protect us from the Wendigo."

"You were the oracle, who could follow the signs," Ibrahim guessed.

Eden nodded. "That's what they called me. And then we had my Tommy, my good and faithful boy. He said he wanted to write a book about our journey. But I think all he really wanted was to be close to me."

"Who wouldn't?" Fred snickered, but Ibrahim silenced him with a judgmental glare.

"But fifty years!" Eden lamented. "What will happen when I get home? Will anyone from my own time–will anyone–remember me?"

"There might be a lot of people who remember you."

"But they'll all be fifty years older. All my friends, all my family! And some of them–maybe all of them–maybe all of them will be dead!"

Ibrahim reached out to Eden's shoulder again, and this time Eden swiftly tumbled herself into his arms. Ibrahim gaped with momentary amazement, and then protectively folded a blanket over his shoulders to cover them both.

Ghazwan closed his eyes and shook his head.

Fred grumbled something about how Ibrahim always gets everything he wants, and he dropped his bowl and spoon into the stew pot with a deliberate clatter. Then he stood and pulled on his parka and his boots.

"Where are you going?" asked Ghazwan.

"Nowhere. There's nowhere to go," Fred huffed, and he stomped out of the tent.

Eden curled herself closer into the protective shell of her blanket and Ibrahim's arms. She stretched her head to his shoulder, and whispered in his ear, "You will protect me from him, won't you?"

"Fred is harmless," said Ibrahim, "He'll walk around in circles until he's too cold to be angry. Then he'll come back."

"Not Fred," Eden whispered. She looked toward Ghazwan and said, "Him."

Ghazwan was eating his stew and pretending to pay no attention to Ibrahim and Eden.

"Your brother who left: he is fire. But your brother who sits there, across from us: he is ice. I can see it growing over his heart. Soon the Wendigo will cover him."

"I'm sitting right here, I can hear you," Ghazwan complained.

"I think you have nothing to worry about," Ibrahim promised. "Ghazwan is my brother and a good man. He has been by my side my whole life."

"Another man, an angel-man, stands by his side now," Eden said, as she stared at Ghazwan and pulled the blanket protectively over her head.

"What do you mean?" asked Ghazwan.

Eden sat up straighter and said to Ghazwan, "You last saw the angel-man only seven days ago. A secret meeting, under the grandfather tree. The angel-man whispered in your ear and he gave you a mission, and a weapon, and a promise of reward when you return."

"Seven days ago," said Ghazwan, "we were all at Miranda's house, planning this expedition. The house was full of people. Nobody could have got in there without being seen."

"There's a grandfather tree in Miranda's back yard," Ibrahim observed.

"I can almost see the angel-man," Eden whispered. "Like the image of a memory, floating in the air. A man who gives freely his sweet wine and honey, until you lose your taste for any other food. A man who loves you, and calls you his friend, until you want no other friends but him, and you push everyone else away. And then he holds you, and he keeps you! And he whispers things in your ears, and you do what he tells you to do. He is an angel, as bright and as perfect as an angel, but holds an hourglass in his hand."

"She's crazy, Ibrahim," said Ghazwan. "Fifty years of solitude have driven her crazy."

Eden continued, saying: "The angel-man promised to make you the lord of a great house. With green fields and sweet gardens, and men at your command."

Now Ibrahim's interest grew. "Do you mean our old madrasa, down in Niagara? The one the Guardians took from us last year?"

"I'm telling you, Ibrahim, she's seeing things, she's crazy," Ghazwan laughed.

Eden added one last note: "And he told you, 'if you want it, then kill the old man'."

Now Ghazwan stood up. "That's enough, you damned liar!" he howled at her.

Eden burrowed herself deeper into Ibrahim's breast, and pulled the blankets over her face.

"An angel with an hourglass. That's the crest of House DiAngelo," Ibrahim said, as he glowered at Ghazwan with suspicion, and petted Eden's hair.

"You can't believe anything she says!" Ghazwan insisted. "We found her up here, half mad from the isolation and half dead from the cold. She can't possibly know anything."

"But what if she *does* know something?" said Ibrahim. "What if she's an oracle? What if that's the reason she was on last expedition, fifty years ago? She helped them find the old man's monastery; she can help us find it, too."

"Now you're just as crazy as she is," Ghazwan accused. "I agreed to come on this fool's errand of yours because you are my brother and you asked for my help. How dare you accuse me of plotting against you!"

Eden carefully peeked her face out from under the blankets and said, "The angel-man gave you a weapon, and it's hidden somewhere in this tent."

Ibrahim glared at Ghazwan. Now there was an accusation in the air that could be proven or disproven by the evidence. Ghazwan sputtered with frustration, and tried to articulate an objection, but Ibrahim didn't wait to hear it. He let go of Eden, and began searching the tent: under the blankets on the floor, under the sleds, behind the food boxes and other supplies, and even inside the layers of the tent walls, while Ghazwan pleaded with him to stop. Inside a burlap sack full of lentils for their stew, Ibrahim found the long black a stiletto, a translucent obsidian blade, and the crest of House DiAngelo engraved on its hand guard.

"So, my enemy sent my own brother to kill the old man," Ibrahim spoke, soft and controlled.

"I didn't put that there," Ghazwan pleaded.

"But still, here it is," Ibrahim stated.

"It might have been her who put it there–maybe that's how she knew it was here!"

"She has been sitting here beside me the whole time."

"You cannot possibly believe her, instead of me! Your own brother!"

"That's an act of desperation, not an argument."

"Ibrahim, I am not your enemy!"

Then Ibrahim shouted, "If you kill the old man, you will be!"

Ghazwan had no reply for Ibrahim's threat. He stared at his brother angrily for a moment, and then turned away. "Dammit, Ibrahim, Eden is right," he confessed.

Eden scuttled away from Ghazwan as far as she could, and pressed her back against a tent pole.

Ibrahim crouched down next to his brother and said, "I know. But I'm glad to hear you say it. Because we have no secrets from each other now. So who was it? Who put you up to it?"

"He didn't tell me his name," Ghazwan explained. "He said he was a member of that first expedition fifty years ago. We talked for a while about what it was like. He gave me that journal. He told me what the old man was really like, in the days before he disappeared. Then he gave me the dagger. And ten thousand dollars! And he said there would be more money for me, and that the Guardians would make me the head of our old madrasa, and we could all go home. But the old man had to die. That was all he wanted me to do."

Ibrahim sat back and said, "So. They offered you money. And they offered to give back the home they stole from us. And you decided to take it - is that how you are! You have to ask yourself if that's the price of your integrity."

"It's not about the money, Ibrahim! Though God knows we need it."

"All right then, if it isn't the money, then what is it!"

Ghazwan struggled to answer, but couldn't. Instead he blurted: "It's the power, it's the freedom, that money can buy. You need money to do just about anything. And the more of it you have, the more you can do. Money is freedom. And I'll tell you something else about money. It's that any man can be bought, if only you can pay his price. Even men like you, Ibrahim! You say you have integrity. You say you don't care about money. That just means your price is very *high*!"

"I'm not against money, Ghazwan. I'm against killing people to get it."

Ghazwan looked away and shook his head. "You're such an idealist, Ibrahim. You just don't understand the hard facts of life."

"Well, I hope that you'll be happy with your money," Ibrahim finished. "Because that's all they're really offering you. Money, in exchange for the death of the wisest and greatest sage of our time."

"That's just what *you* say he is."

"Wouldn't you rather find out for yourself? Wouldn't you rather have a chance–even if it's only a chance–to hear the words of a man who finally discovered who we are, and what this ridiculous rat-race life of ours is truly and finally for? Isn't that worth more than any amount of money? Or do you think that money can clean a dead man's blood from your hands?"

Eden moved around the edge of the tent, and clung to Ibrahim's back, so that he was between her and Ghazwan. Into Ibrahim's ear she whispered, "Don't let him touch me."

Ghazwan glared at Ibrahim for a moment, and then pulled on his parka and reached for his boots.

"Where are you going," Ibrahim said. It was not a question.

"To see that Fred hasn't frozen to death out there," Ghazwan answered. And just before stepping into the winter, he put in his last word: "Anyway, looks like you and your new girlfriend would like some privacy for a while."

Ibrahim clenched his fists, and inhaled sharply. He leapt to his feet and planted himself between Ghazwan and the door.

"Out of my way, Ibrahim," Ghazwan growled.

Eden touched Ibrahim's hand. "Don't, Ibrahim, whatever you're going to do, please don't!"

Ibrahim looked upon Eden, and his anger softened. Then he looked to Ghazwan and said, "If you really must leave, then I want you to take this blade with you." He handed Ghazwan the stiletto.

"What the hell?" said Ghazwan.

"I'm putting this blade in your hand to give you a chance to do the right thing. If all you want is the Guardians' money then you can take it and stab me in my sleep, and then murder the old man, too. But if I am right, and if you really are the good man I believe you are, then you will break this blade in ten pieces and bury it in the snow. I'm putting it in your hands, to show you that I trust you."

Ghazwan stared at Ibrahim, saying nothing, for a moment. Then he sat down on the floor again, and threw one of his boots across the tent.

"Dammit, Ibrahim, what am I going to do with you?

"Good man," Ibrahim laughed. Then he stood and offered his brother his hand and said, "Now let's both go outside and see if we can find Fred."

Ghazwan reluctantly accepted Ibrahim's hand, and got up to his feet.

Eden moved closer and said, "Stay with me, don't go!"

"We'll be gone only a moment," said Ibrahim. "You'll be safe here."

"Please!" Eden cried. "What if it's only a moment for you, but fifty years for me?"

Ibrahim and Ghazwan looked at each other.

Ghazwan said, "But what if it's been fifty years for Fred?"

"Please!" Eden called out.

"Come with us, then," Ibrahim said to Eden. "We'll all stay together."

Eden looked at the pot of stew on the cooker in the middle of the tent, and the little blue kerosene flame beneath it, and she remembered how cold it was outside. The thought of fifty years of solitude moved her to reach for her parka.

\*     \*     \*

They found Fred not far away, staring at the sky. They called to him, but he did not answer; and when they came close to him, they saw why. In the distance, not high above the horizon, a trail of blue-green fire weaved and flowed over the sky.

"Do you think it might be a sign? Are we getting close?" said Ibrahim, excitedly.

"It's just the northern lights," said Ghazwan. "It's not a sign of anything."

Fred spoke quietly to everyone and no one. "I've never seen the northern lights before. My god, they're beautiful. No one ever told me they were beautiful. And you know, I've been standing here and thinking: how can people possibly not see that the world is full of such wonderful things? "

The four seekers watched the lights together for a while.

"Feeling better now about following me up here, Fred?" asked Ibrahim.

Fred only glowered at him, and then said, "It's too cold out here to enjoy the show." He started walking back to the tent.

Eden, with her eyes on the horizon, said, "It's a sign."

Fred turned around.

"The northern lights?" he asked.

"No, the northern darkness," she answered, and she pointed to a frontier of spruces and pines in the middle distance. The brothers looked where she was pointing, and saw only the field of snow, and the trees swaying in a gentle night wind.

"There!" Eden whispered, and she pointed to a shadow that drifted from one tree to another.

"What is it?" asked Ibrahim.

"The Wendigo," she named the shadow. Then she pointed in another direction, where another shadow wafted between two trees. "They are drawn to places of power, just like we are," she explained.

The brothers stepped closer to each other, and looked out in all directions.

"Are they dangerous? Are they going to attack?" said Fred.

"Yes, they are very dangerous," said Eden, "but they will not attack you if you do not have what they want."

"So what do they want?" asked Ibrahim.

"They want to melt the ice on their hearts. But they think the only way to do that is to eat the hearts of others," Eden explained. "But it doesn't help them. Each heart they eat only makes them hunger for more."

Another shadow moved from one tree to another, this time a little faster, and a little closer to where the brothers stood. Ghazwan brandished his stiletto. Fred looked at Ghazwan and wordlessly asked where the weapon came from. Ghazwan shrugged and said nothing, and watched the forest again. Fred broke a branch off a nearby tree and held it defensively.

Ibrahim said, "Maybe we should go back to our tent."

Ghazwan agreed with a nod, and added, "Quietly."

Everyone crept back toward their tent. They winced with the sound of the snow that they crushed under their boots with every step, and they took turns peeking behind them, to see if any shadows followed them.

Someone cracked a fallen tree branch beneath his boot. All eyes looked toward the sound, and then back to the trees, thick with floating shadows. There they saw only stillness, but a stillness that was somehow more menacing than movement.

"I think they know we're here now," whispered Ghazwan.

"Okay then, on the count of three-" said Ibrahim. His brothers did not wait for him to start counting. They ran for the tent, and kicked a flurry of snow into the air behind them. Ibrahim saw two, maybe three, of the shadows swooping toward him. Their shapes grew more distinct now: they were tall, some as much as twice Ibrahim's own stature, and they wore only the tattered remains of their winter boots and cloaks. The tallest of them glowered at Ibrahim with ice-white pits instead of eyes.

Ibrahim howled out involuntarily, and grabbed Eden's wrist and sprinted after his brothers.

\*     \*     \*

Inside the tent, everyone piled their supply packs and food coolers by the door, although they knew it was probably a useless gesture. Two thin layers of canvass and tarpaulin was all that protected them from the winter outside, and from whatever unfeeling and hungry things might be moving from the trees and surrounding them. Ghazwan sat closest to the door, with the stiletto in his hand, and a brave look on his face. Fred sat next to him, with his tree branch ready. Eden sat in the back of the tent, where she covered herself with as many blankets as she could find. Ibrahim frantically scanned the pages of Tommy's journal.

"Ibrahim, what are you doing? Help us build a barricade!" Fred shouted at his brother.

"I'm trying to find out how to fight those things," Ibrahim shot back.

"You cannot fight them," said Eden.

"How did you survive them last time?" asked Fred.

"We didn't," Eden told him. "Not all of us."

"Then what can we do?" said Ghazwan.

Eden seemed not have heard Ghazwan's question. She crawled beside Ibrahim, and whispered again, "Don't let them touch me, don't let them near me."

Ghazwan sighed and rolled his eyes. Fred thumped his stick on the floor impatiently.

Ibrahim asked Eden, "What did you do last time to survive? How did you escape from them?"

"You cannot escape them. They always find you. They always surround and follow you, and they take you, if you have what they want," Eden whispered.

Ghazwan "But you said what they want is to eat people! So - it's like we can't do anything!"

Eden did not respond. She had completely covered herself in her furs and blankets, and she clung to Ibrahim's side.

"Well, if she can't help us, then what does the book say?" asked Fred.

Ghazwan took the book from Ibrahim and thumbed through it for a moment, and then reported, "It seems they barricaded themselves in their camp, just like we did. Then nothing happened, so they all went to sleep. The writer here guessed that those creatures could not get too close to the light. But when everyone woke in the morning, some of them were missing. And there was blood on the snow."

Eden's face emerged from beneath her blanket, and she said, "Someone found a dagger in Tommy's pack, that night. He said wasn't his. But some of them men didn't believe him. And those who did believe him, they accused others of plotting secret murder. I remember there was a lot of shouting, and more knives were found in hidden places, and then there was more shouting. I took all the blankets I could carry and ran into the woods with Tommy. We went back when we were hungry. But all the men were gone. Some scattered and ran away. Some were dead on the snow."

The brothers contemplated Eden's story.

"I guess no one here goes to sleep tonight," Ghazwan stated.

Ibrahim reached out to both his brothers and said, "There's a bright side to all this."

"Your optimism is getting annoying," Fred grumbled.

Ibrahim ignored him, and said, "If we're surrounded by creatures of the mythic age, it means we're getting close to a place of power. Maybe we're getting close to where the old man himself made his new home! We just have to survive this night, and then get through the forest tomorrow."

"The forest full of Wendigo," Fred reminded him.

"We'll do it during the day when it's safer," Ibrahim told Fred. "If we start early in the morning, and follow the map, we should get there by sunset. If we ration our food, we'll still have enough for the journey home. We're so close now, we're so close! The forest outside may be full of danger. But we are protected and safe in this shelter. Any place where men like us gather and raise a flag becomes a house of safety and peace. Now, let us face the Holy City and make the Night Prayer. Let us read as much of the Quran as may be easy. Tomorrow we will come to the end of our struggle. Our questions shall be answered. It shall be a good day."

As Ibrahim unrolled his prayer mat and faced what he guessed was southeast, Fred and Ghazwan looked at each other.

"I'm as much a part of the Ummah as he is," Ghazwan whispered. "I won't have him telling me what to do."

Fred shifted his body to turn his back on Ibrahim, and then leaned toward his brother to speak more secretly. "Ghazwan, suppose we find the old man. Then, suppose that Ibrahim decides he doesn't like what the old man has to say. What do you think he will do?"

"That is an excellent question," Ghazwan acknowledged. "At the very least, I'm sure he won't be happy."

"I know what he'll do," said Fred. "He'll declare that the old man is a fake. He'll say that the real man is still out there somewhere, and we still have to find him. And he will never let us go home."

"You're probably right," Ghazwan agreed.

"I'll tell you what he'll do to this woman we found today. He'll say that she's no oracle, and that she's a fake, as well. And he'll abandon her in the winter, where she will probably freeze to death."

"He wouldn't dare! He knows the ways of our people. He would not leave someone in the desert like that!"

"Yes, he would. Look at him! His mind has become one-pointed. He knows no other reality but the one that he imagines. Much like men who took our freehold away. Eventually, he will find that the world does not conform to his expectations. And when that happens, I would like to be very far away."

Ghazwan looked to Ibrahim, who was praying in a corner of the tent, with his back to his two brothers. Eden sat next to him, and watched him pray.

Ghazwan turned to Fred and whispered, "If anyone has ice growing over his heart, it's him. What do you think we should do?"

Fred sighed, and said, "Tonight, we let him believe whatever he wants to believe. And tomorrow, when he is busy talking to the old man, we look around, see if there's a flying boat, or a seven-league-door, or whatever the old man used to find his way up here. And we take it, and we go home."

"What if the old man walked up here, just like we're doing now?"

"Then we make sure we pack all the food in our sleds, and we start walking south, when Ibrahim isn't looking."

"What about Ibrahim?"

"He'll have his quest to find the old man. That will keep him happy."

"Eden?"

"If she wants to come with us, we take her."

"And if we invite her to come, but she warns Ibrahim instead?"

Fred snapped at him: "Do you want to go home, or not?"

"Of course I do," Ghazwan admitted.

"Well, then, you know what we have to do."

Ghazwan folded his hands under his chin thoughtfully, and then turned to look at Ibrahim and Eden. He drew his dagger into hiding under his blankets, and tapped its hilt as if to assure himself it would remain hidden there.

Fred saw him do it, so he asked, "Well, that's interesting. Where did you get it?"

"Oh, you know. I found it lying around Miranda's house, when we were getting ready to go. The North is full of monsters. That's why it's madness to go there. So I thought it might be useful, for protection," Ghazwan smiled.

Eden, quietly sitting across the floor, saw where Ghazwan had hidden it. She looked away, lest Ghazwan guess that she had seen where he hid it.

Ibrahim finished praying, and he returned to his brothers and said, "Well now, my brothers. The hour is late. I recommend we dim the lantern, and get as much sleep as we can. But let's take turns keeping watch. Ghazwan, you should go first."

"Why me?" Ghazwan complained.

"Because, as I said before, I trust you."

Ghazwan closed his eyes, and sighed, and then said, "I'll wake you in three hours for the second watch."

"Very good," Ibrahim agreed.

Ibrahim laid out his blankets and pillows on his sled. Eden pulled her blankets closer around her. Then Ibrahim offered to Eden his sled to sleep upon, so she would not have to lie on a mere carpet on the cold earth. She smiled for him, and touched his hand thankfully, and lay down. Ibrahim bundled himself on the floor beside her, and satisfied himself that the small kindness he showed her was all he needed to keep himself warm. Fred wrapped himself in his own blankets, and stretched himself on his belly, on his sled. Ghazwan pulled another blanket over his shoulders to keep warm, and then dimmed the lantern, and sat by the entrance to the tent. He picked up Tommy's journal to read while he passed the time.

\*   \*   \*

Some hours later, when he thought everyone was sleeping, Ghazwan crept closer to Eden. He hovered over her face, and drew back the blanket on her shoulder as much as he dared. He did not want to wake her, but he wanted to touch her, and smell her breath, and be near her. After a moment he withdrew, and took up a length of rope, and peeled Eden's blankets back again.

Across the tent, Fred was disturbed from his sleep by the sound of Ghazwan's movements. He opened his eyes, and saw what Ghazwan was doing. His first instinct was to say something to make him stop. Then it occurred to him that Ghazwan's dagger was unattended. Quietly, slowly, secretly, Fred reached over to Ghazwan's blankets, and slipped the dagger into a new hiding place, within reach of his own hand. Then he cleared his throat, to let Ghazwan know he was watched.

Ghazwan swiftly snapped his fingers away from Eden, and looked on his brother and ground his teeth. Then he decided it was better to go back to his seat by the lamp, near the entrance to the tent.

Fred closed his eyes and pretended to sleep again, and he stifled the smile on his face.

\*   \*   \*

Ghazwan didn't notice that his blade was missing until the following morning, when everyone was striking the camp. As his search grew more frantic, Ibrahim asked him what he was doing. He didn't want to admit that the blade was lost, so he said there was a lump in his bed last night and he wanted to find out what it was. Ibrahim grinned and returned to his own business. Ghazwan took his bedding out of the tent and shook it, to see what might fall out, but nothing did, so he shook out the rugs on the tent floor next. Fred smiled knowingly. Eden whispered that the ice on his heart was growing thicker.

When the camp was almost fully packed into the sleds, Ghazwan gave up looking for the stiletto. He turned to his younger brother and said, "So, Ibrahim, which way does your magic eye say we should go today?"

"It says we should keep going north, nothing more," Ibrahim reported. He looked to Eden and said, "How did your expedition find the old man's hideout?"

Eden looked into the distance as she answered, "The summoner told us to go north from here, and that we would find a line of stone cairns in the woods. They will show you the rest of the way."

"That sounds easy," Fred grinned.

Eden dropped her packs and said, "The stones will lead you to the centre of the winter."

"We're already in the middle of winter!" Ghazwan sniggered.

"You are only in the beginning of the winter," Eden clarified. "Not all of you will reach the end."

Ibrahim stepped toward her and said, "How do you know?"

Eden didn't answer. Instead she continued to stare into the distance.

"What's the matter with her?" said Ghazwan.

"She's an oracle," Ibrahim guessed. "Maybe she's having a vision."

"It's happening again!" Eden whispered, and then she grabbed her fallen pack and flew back inside the tent.

"Yup, she's an oracle," said Fred. "Crazy as the rest of them."

Ghazwan moved to the front of the tent and called to Eden, "Come out, please, we have to take the tent down and start moving."

"No," cried Eden.

"What's the matter? What are you afraid of?"

"It's happening again!"

"What's happening again?"

"The men with the ice on their hearts are coming!"

Ghazwan laughed. "It's a sunny and beautiful day today! You yourself told us the Wendigo prefer the dark."

Ibrahim nudged Ghazwan and said, "Maybe you should let me talk to her. After all, she thinks you are a Wendigo."

Eden was almost hysterical now. "The sun will go dark today, and the men with the ice in their hearts will come," she shrieked.

Ghazwan's voice became more stern. "We don't have time to hide from them, Eden! We can't wait another day or we won't have enough food to get home. We have to find the old man today, and before nightfall. You have to show us the way!"

"I don't want to go!" Eden howled.

"We don't have time for this!" Ghazwan growled, and he took Eden by the wrist and tried to pull her out of the tent.

"Ghazwan, what are you doing!" Ibrahim shouted.

Ghazwan did not reply. He pulled Eden out of the yurt by her ankles, and dropped her in a nearby snowbank. Then he rushed to undo the knots and ropes that held the tent together. Eden screamed at him, and tried to strike him with one of the tent poles. Ghazwan easily wrestled it out of her hands, and then tried to grasp her with both his arms around her waist and carry her away. Eden thrashed and flailed her arms and legs about, but her effort was useless: Ghazwan's arms were too strong for her. Fred and Ibrahim looked at each other, each waiting for the other to say or do something first. When Eden threw both her arms up in the air and began to slide down and out of her parka, the brothers ran to Eden's rescue. Fred tried to catch Eden in his arms before she fell into the snow. Ibrahim grabbed Ghazwan's hood and jerked him roughly back, and then put his arms under and around Ghazwan's shoulders, and his hands behind Ghazwan's head. Ghazwan was forced to let Eden go. She landed in Fred's arms, but Fred was not quite ready to take her weight, and he fell on his back. Eden slipped entirely out of her parka. Now she had only her boots and snowpants and a cotton shirt to protect her from the winter. She screamed at Ghazwan again, and hurled a few handfuls of snow at his face, and then grabbed her parka and ran away.

"Eden!" shouted Ghazwan. He tried to run after her, but Ibrahim would not let him. The two brothers wrestled for a while, as Ghazwan shouted Eden's name and uselessly reached for her. Then Fred joined the effort to hold Ghazwan to the ground, until he finally stopped fighting them. They watched Eden run until she jumped into a copse of cedar trees and was out of sight. Ghazwan called out Eden's name one last time. Eden made no reply. When Fred and Ibrahim decided that Eden was far enough away, they let Ghazwan push them away.

Ghazwan turned to his brothers and howled, "You traitors! You God-damned dog-fucking traitors! You think you are such Rambos, to hold me down like that. Two against one!"

Ibrahim took a few steps after Eden, but then stopped, and leaned on the walls of the stone crevasse. "You are the traitor, Ghazwan! She was the oracle, she could have taken us to the end! And you chased her away! And why were you in such a rush to get moving? Did you want her to help us find the old man, so you could learn from him, or so you could kill him?"

"What are you talking about?" said Fred.

"That's the real reason he came with us," Ibrahim explained. "Someone paid him to murder the old man."

Fred looked at Ghazwan and said, "Is that the real reason you had that dagger?"

Ghazwan admitted, "I don't have it anymore. I lost it last night. I thought that maybe Eden stole it. I don't know where it is."

"Good," said Ibrahim. "I hope you are with us for the right reasons now."

Ghazwan looked away again, in the direction where Eden fled, and then he turned to his brothers and said, "Ibrahim, Fred, I apologize. Truly. It was not right for me to deceive you as I did. I know that when you held me down, you were doing what you thought you had to do. I forgive you both."

"*You* forgive *us*?" Fred sputtered.

Ghazwan shrugged, and looked to the ground.

"Very well," Ibrahim decided. "Now let there be peace between us again." He held out his open hands for his brothers to take, which Ghazwan did, but Fred did not; Fred only returned to the bags he was packing on his sled.

"Let's just get moving," he growled.

"Maybe we should follow her, see that she's safe," Ghazwan suggested.

"Feeling a little guilty, are we?" Fred scolded him.

When Ibrahim let them go, he said, "We don't have to worry about her. She knows the way to the monastery from here, so she will be fine. As for us: we have the map. And the journal. And Eden told us what to look for. We're very close to the end of our journey."

Fred said, "Ibrahim, you surprise me. I thought you would want to chase after Eden. She might die out there."

"She's probably going straight to the old man now," Ibrahim answered. "We're close enough she could get there easily. Tonight we will find her drinking tea in his kitchen. I'm not worried about her at all."

Fred glared at Ibrahim coldly. When Ibrahim saw this, he gestured to Fred to continue helping strike the camp.

"Last night, Ghazwan and I made a decision," said Fred. "If we do not find your old man today, and we mean *to-day*, then we are going home."

"But we are so *close!*" Ibrahim burst out.

"You keep telling us that," Fred swore, "And yet where are all the magical signs that we are supposed to see? So we've seen the northern lights, and a shot from a flare gun, and we've seen our wheels disappear. What else have we seen? Nothing! This holy pilgrimage of yours is a wild goose chase, Ibrahim. I'm through with it!"

"You cannot go home by yourselves," Ibrahim countered. "It is too dangerous. The Wendigo will find you. We have to stay together."

"You keep threatening us with the dangers of the winter, to keep us by your side. Let me tell you, brother, if you cannot deliver us to the old man by tonight, then it won't be you offering your protection to us. It will be us removing our protection from you."

"Look at the map!" Ibrahim shrieked, as he fumbled for the map in his pockets. "There, see. There! Our final destination is less than a day away. And Eden told us what to look for now. We are so close, we are so close!"

Fred and Ghazwan looked at each other.

"You had better be right, this time," Fred growled.

\*　　\*　　\*

The path they followed that day took them into a forest of tall pines and spruces. A gentle bed of new snow lay upon every branch. every branched swayed in a gentle winter breeze, which sometimes let thin veils of snow fly up and scatter across the faces of the seekers. The colours were stark and sharp: the deep green of the pine needles, the pure white of the snow, the black of the shadows, the sea-blue of the sky. Goldfinches, orioles, and cardinals flitted about them, and one landed on a branch near Ibrahim, who laughed with happiness to see it.

"Those are summer birds. What are they doing here, in the middle of winter?" asked Ghazwan.

"We're getting closer. It's a sign," Ibrahim decided.

As Ibrahim spoke, Fred mouthed the words '*It's a sign*' behind his back. Ghazwan saw him do it, and laughed. Ibrahim smiled with him, although he didn't know what his brother was laughing at. This made Ghazwan and Fred laugh louder.

"I'm so glad the unpleasantness of this morning is over," said Ibrahim. "Today shall be a good day."

Fred stopped laughing, and clenched his fists again. Then he removed one of his mittens and checked under his belt, to assure himself that the stiletto was safely hidden there.

\* \* \*

After they had walked for most of the day, the path took them to a tall cairn of stones at the side of a frozen stream. The brother stopped, and dropped the bags they carried on their backs and unhooked the sled-cables from their belts, and rested.

"This must be the cairn that Eden told us to look for," said Ibrahim.

"Look!" said Ghazwan, as he pointed to another cairn, half-hidden among the trees, a short distance away. "So, all we have to do is follow the line of stones, and we're there!"

"My brothers," said Ibrahim, "I thank you, truly, for coming with me all this distance. Tonight your struggles and doubts shall end, I am sure of it."

"We have one more struggle, Ibrahim. Look there," said Fred, and he pointed west. A bank of clouds was rolling toward them, and a blizzard was tumbling in beneath it. As they watched, the clouds covered the sun, and all the shadows under the trees thickened and spread.

"Eden told us that when we found the first cairn, the sun would go dark, and we would come into the center of the winter," Ghazwan observed. "I'd say this blizzard will make her prophesy come true."

"Well Fred, you said you wanted a sign!"

"I was hoping for something less dangerous," Fred replied

"We should put up the tent, right here, before that storm hits," said Ghazwan.

"Too late," said Fred, as he pointed to a suspicious shadow under a nearby tree. "The Wendigo are already too close."

Ibrahim said, "We might still have time to reach the sanctuary before the storm hits us."

The brothers ran. Winter swallowed them anyway.

*   *   *

The trees were smaller in the forest ahead of them, but they stood closer together. The brothers were compelled to run single-file along the path. Ibrahim went first; Fred followed him; and Ghazwan came third in their line. It was not difficult to run, but sometimes they slipped on patches of ice, and sometimes they clambered over the high snow drifts that the wind deposited before them. The narrow path, hedged on each side by the evergreens and cedars, compressed and quickened the wind, and the cold air bit their faces.

Ibrahim was the fastest of the three, and although the others were not far behind him, they soon lost sight of each other. Fred shouted Ibrahim's name, but his voice was smothered in the wind. Fred knew his brother only by the crunch of his snowshoes on the hard snow. Then that, too, disappeared, and Ibrahim was only a track of footprints in the ground. Fred followed the track, and it led to the next cairn in on the trail. He stopped there to catch his breath. Then the heard the sound of new footsteps approaching him from behind.

"Ghazwan?" he called out.

But the figure which emerged from the winter was a tall and lanky monstrosity, half-covered in a rotting fur coat. Its cold white eyes, devoid of human presence, bore down on Fred. Fred shrieked and drew his hidden stiletto. The Wendigo hissed at Fred and raised a heavy tree branch, to club Fred down. Fred decided it was better to flee than to fight. He used his stiletto to cut the cables of the sled he was pulling, and then dashed away, following the track of Ibrahim's steps as best he could.

When he reached the next cairn, he thought he was far enough away from the Wendigo to slow down and catch his breath again. When he was ready to move on, he turned to follow Ibrahim's trail again, but found a dark shape in his path. It was about the same height as himself, and facing away from him, and as Fred watched the shape crouched down and sit in the snow.

"Ibrahim?" asked Fred.

The shape made no reply, but Fred could see it more clearly now. The figure had wide shoulders and long limbs, and a warm turban adorned with stars and moons.

"Ibrahim!" Fred shouted. Still the figure did not move.

Fred decided that Ibrahim was succumbing to the cold, and couldn't reply. Then he remembered he was still holding the stiletto in his hand. He looked backwards for a moment, to see if the creature was still following him. Although he could see no further than a few meters with any clarity, he satisfied himself that he was no longer in danger. Then he crept toward Ibrahim as slowly and quietly as he could. He trusted the winter to help muffle his footsteps. He paused when he was half way there, and looked over his shoulder again. Then he considered his mark, just under Ibrahim's shoulders. Or perhaps he could leap forward and plunge the blade around in front, and into Ibrahim's heart.

Then he decided all that he needed to do was tell Ibrahim he was leaving. He kept the blade raised in a fighting stance, to show Ibrahim he was serious. He gripped the blade tighter, and held his breath, and poked his brother in the shoulder.

Ibrahim flashed to the side just in time. Fred lost balance and almost fell into the snow. When he regained his footing he saw that it was not Ibrahim, but Eden, whom he had attacked. She removed the turban from her head with a flourish, and her brown hair tumbled out, thick and long, and flew free in the wind. Her posture showed none of the fear and fragility that defined her when the brothers first found her. The way she held her summoner's staff told Fred that she could disarm and disable him if she wanted to.

"How did you–!" Fred began to say. Then he fully grasped the new image of Eden he was seeing, and he said, "Who are you *really*!"

"I told you my name," said Eden. "But what I did not tell you is that I am the Summoner."

"You? No! You're not the summoner! You can't be!"

Eden only laughed at him. "Your world view must be very simple, indeed."

"So you're not a survivor of that other expedition, fifty years ago?"

"Actually, yes, I am. I became the Elder's Summoner only a short while later. And I know perfectly well what year it is, and how much time has passed."

"So you lied to us!"

"I allowed you to believe what you wanted to believe. The better for me to observe the kind of men you really are."

With a gesture to the sky from Eden, the heaviness of the blizzard lightened somewhat, allowing Fred to see further around him.

Fred smirked and said, "All right then. What kind of man do you say I am?"

"You're a loyal man, and curious, and thoughtful. But also resentful. Hateful. Angry."

"No, I'm not!" Fred shouted.

"You told your brother directly that you hate him. And just now, you wanted to kill him!"

"I did not!"

"And what is more, you were planning it, last night. That is why you took the dagger from Ghazwan."

Fred looked at the weapon in his hand, and knew that Eden was right.

Eden said, "But be at peace, Frederick Nefzawi. No seekers of good heart are ever turned away from the sanctuary. Especially in weather like this."

"Seekers of good heart," Fred repeated. "And yet you say I am hateful and resentful."

"I also say you are loyal and thoughtful. I have heard you ask questions: good and serious questions. I have an elderly friend who has all the same questions as you. I think you might like to meet him. He is expecting you."

"You mean, the old man? He's expecting me?"

Eden nodded, and said: "And so you have a choice, young man. You can turn back, and try to find your brothers. Maybe try to kill them again. Or, you can choose to throw down your blade and leave your hate behind, here in the snow."

Fred stepped backwards, away from Eden, and then looked down the path where he came from.

"What you ask is impossible! A man can't change who he is, just like that," Fred argued.

"You're right," Eden agreed. "You can't change your whole nature in a single magic moment. But what you can do, in each moment, is make a decision, right now, about what you will or will not do. In your case, you can decide, right now, what to do with that blade in your hand."

Eden smiled at Fred one last time, and then stepped down the path toward the next cairn, and the old man's monastery. The wind picked up a little bit, and more snow whipped up into the air again, and Eden vanished into it, leaving only her footprints behind.

Fred stood alone in the storm, as the cold seeped into his parka, and the weight of his decision grew harder to bear. The driving snow was covering Eden's footprints; Fred feared he would be stranded if they vanished entirely. He looked at the stiletto in his hand, and traced his finger on the heraldic symbols on its hilt. Then he hurled it into the ground, and stepped forth, following Eden's footsteps.

The blizzard cleared as he walked on, and Fred soon found himself standing on the shore of a small frozen lake, with a rocky island emerging from its centre. Its cliffs were not high, but they were steep and sharp, with knots of hanging green vines, and streams of clear fresh water tumbling into pools and falls, and summer birds flying around it. A slight mist circled its base, where the cold dry air of winter met the warm and rich air of the summer, making it seem as if the island floated on a cloud. A stairway cut into the cliffside led to a cluster of small round stone huts on a plateau. On the summit of the hill stood two trees, mightier and greener than all others, one full of bright spring flowers, the other full of summer berries.

* * *

Ghazwan also lost sight of his brothers in the blizzard. He tried his best to follow the path made by the cairns, and the footsteps of those who went ahead of him. This took him to a clearing in the woods, sheltered somewhat by a hedge of cedars and a slight depression in the earth. Five tents occupied the clearing, although most of them were collapsed or covered in rot. One was completely shredded as a tree had fallen over it. Ghazwan decided to shelter himself in the one that seemed most intact, and wait for the end of the blizzard. Just inside it he discovered the frozen and mummified remains of a man. He jerked his hand back, and stepped away.

That is when he saw Eden, standing by the edge of the campsite, watching him.

"There you are!" Ghazwan called to her.

With a gesture of Eden's hand, the blizzard partially abated, just enough to allow the two of them to talk more easily.

"Is this your old camp?" Ghazwan asked. "From your expedition, fifty years ago? If it is, would you mind if I stayed here for a while? Until the storm passes?"

Eden moved toward him now, with slow and deliberate steps.

Ghazwan pointed to the body he had uncovered and said, "Was this someone from your expedition? Was this your friend who wrote the journal?"

"His name was Orazio Maliguida," said Eden. "He was one of the scholars who had questions for the Elder. Or that's what he told us."

"What happened to him?" Ghazwan asked. He crouched down before the body and looked into its face for a moment. Then he brushed away some more snow around it. He found that the body was hugging a wooden lockbox in his arms, and holding a stiletto in his hands, much like the one Ghazwan had been given by his paymaster. Ghazwan sat back, as he realized the answer to his own question.

"I'm sorry about what I did earlier. I didn't want to frighten you," he said to Eden.

Eden stood just outside the reach of Ghazwan's arms, and planted her staff in the snow in front of her defensively.

"I'm not a Wendigo. You don't have to be afraid of me," Ghazwan reassured her.

Ghazwan could she was not afraid of him anyway, and her defiant posture made him feel the cold a little closer to his flesh. He took Orazio's dagger, and he scrambled behind one of the tents, and held up the weapon defensively.

"You're not just another scout, are you!" he shouted. "And how did you know about my dagger, anyway? Did Paul Turner put you up to this? You're from the Guardians too, aren't you! You're here to make sure the job gets done! Well, look, I've got a new dagger now. I can still do it."

Eden said, "That's not why I'm here."

"You want to do the job yourself! So you can get the money instead of me!"

Eden laughed and said, "No, no, no."

Ghazwan kept his dagger pointed at her, and tried to think. Quickly he hit upon the only other possible explanation, although he didn't like it: "You're the summoner!"

Eden nodded. "I'm a scout of the Orenda Nation. And, yes, I am the summoner."

"I promise you, I'm not a Wendigo," Ghazwan pleaded.

"You're going to become one, very soon."

Ghazwan stepped back, and then angrily stepped forward again. "Why do you keep saying that!"

"Because I've seen the kind of man you are," Eden told him. "You're a man of divided loyalties. You love your brothers, you love your House. But you love yourself, more. You have fire inside you, but you also have ice, and they fight each other inside you. If it's the ice that wins, then you will become a Wendigo."

"Ibrahim said you were an oracle," Ghazwan muttered. "Never liked oracles, myself. Always crying about the future you can see but never change. Always angry because no one ever believes you. Always complaining that your gift is a curse."

"Actually, I don't think it's a curse at all," Eden smiled. "I like being the first to know what's going to happen. I like being prepared."

"So, you say that can you see my soul? Do you know exactly when I'm supposed to become a Wendigo? Are you here to kill me before that happens?"

Eden laughed. "No."

"Then why are you here?"

"To lead you to the monastery. The Elder is expecting you."

Ghazwan stepped back, and struggled for words for a moment. "Why would you do that? Aren't you afraid I'll turn into some kind of monster?"

"You should fear that, more than me."

"Ha!" Ghazwan dismissed her words. Then he looked around and said, "I'm going to look around here first. There might be a few things here I can still use."

"Take only what you can carry," Eden told him, and she started to walk away.

Ghazwan looked around. In one of the tents he found the previous expedition's food cache. Everything that was not kept in tins had spoiled, or had been eaten by animals, in the intervening years. And the tins were so covered in rust that he didn't trust them. In another tent he found a roll of blankets, but they too had rotted with age. Then his curiosity about the lockbox in Orazio's arms returned to him. He broke the lock with a stone, and opened it. Inside he found a leather purse which contained more than a dozen tarnished coins. He polished one clean with his fingers, and saw that it bore the image of a bearded man on one side, and a wheat stalk on the other.

"Gold clutches! From the Secret City of Uttarakhand. This is a small fortune!"

Beneath the coin purse was a scroll, tied with a ribbon. Ghazwan opened it, and found that it was a contract to assassinate the Old Man.

"There must be a lot of people who would pay to see the old fellow dead. I could really cash in with this," he said aloud. Eden did not answer; she was standing a distance away, waiting for him to be done.

Ghazwan put everything back in the box again, and closed it. Then he re-attached the sled cables to his belt, picked the box up in his arms, and followed Eden toward the monastery.

The blizzard cleared, and Ghazwan found himself at the edge of a small frozen lake, with the old man's island in the center. Ghazwan laughed with relief at having reached it. Eden smiled, and crossed the ice ahead of him. Ghazwan jumped after her enthusiastically.

His first step caused the ice to crack, and he plunged up to his ankles in the cold water. He jumped back, and then tried again more carefully. But the ice still did not support him: on his second attempt it cracked again, only a few meters from the shore, and he was stuck in the ice up to his knees. He threw the box into a snowbank on the shore and clawed his way back.

"Hey there, Eden! Can you help me with this?" he shouted. Eden did not seem to hear him. She floated lightly across the ice, and the mist at the island's edge hid her from his sight.

Ghazwan sat on a nearby stone, and looked back and forth for a while at his sled, the box of letters and coins, and the ice, and the island. He considered attaching the box to his sled, but then decided that might weigh the sled down too much as well. As the blizzard winds gusted stronger, and it seemed the island would soon disappear, Ghazwan remembered the last thing Eden told him, and he made a decision. He detached the sled cables from his belt, and stashed the sled and the box under a nearby tree, and tied them to the tree with some extra rope. He stepped on to the ice without them. It held his weight.

He jumped up and down a few times, just to be sure, and the ice still held him. He smiled. Then he walked out a short distance, and turned to see how easily he could find his sled again. The blizzard returned, and began covering them with a fresh film of snow, and Ghazwan quickly realized that if he left them behind, he could cross the ice to the island with no trouble, but he would almost certainly never find his chest of gold again.

He opened his treasure chest and pocketed the coin purse in one of his boots, and the dagger in the other, and then set out over the ice again. The ice held his weight. As he walked he laughed, for he thought he had found a loophole in Eden's cryptic warning. As the outline of the jagged island grew clearer, and the wind lessened and brought to him the songs of summer birds and the scents of spring flowers, he laughed again, and jogged ahead.

Then he heard the thunder of the ice cracking behind him. He stopped laughing, and ran.

\*     \*     \*

Ibrahim came to the edge of the lake on his own, by following the line of the cairns. Eden met him there. As the blizzard cleared somewhat and his eyes could take in the full height of the island-mountain in the lake, and its two trees, he smiled, and then he laughed, and then he threw handfuls of snow in the air and laughed again.

"The Elder is expecting you," said Eden.

When Ibrahim set out over the ice, his sled immediately cracked the ice beneath it, and fell into the water. Ibrahim hauled it on to the shore, and detached its cables from his belt.

"I suppose I won't need this anyway," he said of it. But he unpacked his flag, and brandished it high as he crossed the lake again.

"You won't need that either," said Eden. "The Elder knows who you are."

Ibrahim glared at her and said, "I have come a long way. I have earned the right to carry my flag. I shall greet the old man as one lord of a great house to another."

He set forth over the ice again. When he reached the foot of the island, he grinned, and pulled off his mittens so he could touch the warm streams falling from the cliffs. He picked a nearby lavender and enjoyed its perfume, and he kissed the stones reverently. Then he climbed the first few steps to the plateau and called out: "I call upon the fabled Lord of this freehold, he who is known as the Old Man! I am Ibrahim Nefzawi, the caliph of the Songhais of Niagara, and I call upon you to admit me into your realm!"

Only the echo of his own voice answered him. He called again, but still heard only his echo, and the cries of seagulls whom his voice disturbed.

As he climbed higher, the blizzard raised its breath, and breathed into the summer air of the island. Soon Ibrahim was surrounded by whipping winds and circling snowflakes again.

When he reached what he thought was the edge of the plateau where the old man's monastery lay, Ibrahim shouted out again: "I call to the lord of this freehold! I am Ibrahim Nefzawi, the caliph of House Songhai! I have struggled long, many years, to find you. I come seeking your famous wisdom! If you are as wise and great as all the world says you are, you will open your gate to me! As one lord of a great Hidden House to another, and upon your honour, I summon you!"

The blizzard was now too dense for Ibrahim to see much further ahead than the length of his arm. He stepped forward carefully, and tapped his flag-pole on the ground like a blind man, in case of loose flagstones or hidden foxholes in the ground. His exploration took him to a snowbank, and then past a few tall spruce trees, and then his flagpole struck something hollow and metal.

The blizzard lessened somewhat, and allowed him to see his whereabouts. He found himself standing beside his own pickup truck, which was precariously parked on the side of a highway, and half-buried in the snow.

Ibrahim walked into the centre of the highway, with his hands out before him, as if afraid he would stumble into an invisible wall.

A truck approached. It blasted its horn to warn Ibrahim off the road. When he didn't move, it slowed to a stop, and the driver rolled down his window and said, "Out of gas? Need a lift into town?"

Ibrahim stared at him, wild-eyed and shaking, and did not know how to answer.

*     *     *

That night, the ice near the shore of the old man's island broke from below. A lanky, long-limbed, and decrepit figure, with sunken white eyes, punched its way free of the ice, and swallowed a great gulp of air, and screamed at the world. It tore off most of its winter clothes, as the water that saturated them crackled and froze. A few gold coins fell from one of its boots, as it staggered on to the shore. And when it felt the solid earth beneath its feet, it screamed again, and lurched into the forest, to the south.

*~ the end ~*

## ~ About the Author ~

Brendan Myers is a professor of philosophy at Cégep Heritage College, in Gatineau, Quebec. He is the author of fifteen books, and he lives in a library, next door to a forest.

Find him on the web at http://brendanmyers.net

Follow him on Twitter @Fellwater

*Other titles by Brendan Myers*

*Fiction:*

Fellwater
Hallowstone
Clan Fianna
Jillian Brighton and the Wonderful Cosmographic Telescope

*Non-fiction:*

The Other Side of Virtue
Loneliness and Revelation
Circles of Meaning, Labyrinths of Fear
The Earth, The Gods, and The Soul